W9-BIH-532

To Emma

My Weirder-est School #1: Dr. Snow Has Got to Go!

Text copyright © 2019 by Dan Gutman

Illustrations copyright © 2019 by Jim Paillot

www.harpercollinschildrens.com

ISBN 978-0-06-269101-9 (pbk. bdg.)—ISBN 978-0-06-269102-6 (library bdg.)

Typography by Laura Mock

18 19 20 21 22   CG/LSCH   10 9 8 7 6 5 4 3 2 1

❖

First Edition

My Weirder-est School #1

Dr. Snow Has Got to Go!

Fountaindale Public Library
Bolingbrook, IL
(630) 759-2102

Dan Gutman

**Pictures by
Jim Paillot**

HARPER
An Imprint of HarperCollinsPublishers

Contents

A.J.

RYAN

MICHAEL

XIA

ANDREA

EMILY

NEIL

The *L* Word

My name is A.J. and I *love* peanut butter and jelly sandwiches.

That's right. I *love* peanut butter and jelly sandwiches. And I'm not ashamed to say it out loud, right in the middle of the vomitorium!

"What?!" shouted Michael, who never

ties his shoes. "A.J., did you just say the *L* word?"

"A.J. said the *L* word!" shouted Ryan, who will eat anything, even stuff that isn't food.

"A.J. said the *L* word!" shouted Neil, who we call the nude kid even though he wears clothes.

"A.J. said the *L* word!" shouted Alexia, this girl who rides a skateboard all the time.*

Everybody was staring at me like I had just grown a third eyeball in the middle of my head. They all looked like they were going to faint.

"Big deal," I said. "I love skateboarding. I love playing football. I love my parents. I love pizza."

"I think that's just *wonderful*, Arlo," said Andrea Young, this annoying girl with curly brown hair. She calls me by my real name because she knows I don't like it. "It's *good* to talk about the things

---

*In case you were wondering, everybody was shouting that I said the *L* word.

3

you love. I love school. I love singing and dancing and reading Shakespeare, and learning new things and getting good grades and–"

"Oooh," Ryan said, "A.J. and Andrea are talking about the things they love. They must be in *love*!"

"When are you gonna get married?" asked Michael.

The truth is, I love peanut butter and jelly sandwiches because they are awesome. I love peanut butter. I love jelly. When you put peanut butter and jelly together, they're even more awesome than they were in separate jars.

"Saying the word 'love' out loud means you're becoming more mature, Arlo," said

Andrea. "I'm so glad to hear that you're turning over a new leaf."

What? I didn't turn any leaves over. What do leaves have to do with anything? And why would anybody bother turning over a leaf? Leaves are pretty much the same on both sides, so it's a waste of time to turn them over.

Why can't a truck full of leaves fall on Andrea's head?

STEM

I go to Ella Mentry School. It was named after a rich lady named Ella Mentry, so it has the perfect name: Ella Mentry School. Mrs. Mentry used to be a teacher at our school a long time ago, when dinosaurs walked the earth. After she retired, she donated a million dollars to the school.

Mrs. Mentry is really old now and walks with a cane. She still lives in the neighborhood. So if she forgets her name, she can just walk over to our school and see it on the sign. One time, she came to visit and a food fight broke out in the vomitorium. That was weird.

But last week, the weirdest thing in the history of the world happened. Our teacher, Mr. Cooper, came running into our classroom.

Well, that's not the weird part. Mr. Cooper comes running into our classroom *every* day. The weird part was what happened next—a meteorite crashed through the window, smashed into the whiteboard

in a giant fireball, and knocked Mr. Cooper onto the floor!

Okay, that didn't really happen. But I thought it would be more interesting than saying that Mr. Cooper tripped over his shoelaces. That's what actually happened.

Mr. Cooper thinks he's a superhero, which is why he wears a cape all the time. Only superheroes wear capes. Nobody knows why. But that's the first rule of being a superhero.

"I'm okay!" Mr. Cooper said, jumping to his feet. "Let's start our day, shall we? Turn to page twenty-three in your math books."

Ugh, I hate math. Why do we have to study math? Isn't that why Benjamin Franklin invented the calculator?*

Luckily, we didn't have to do math. Because at that moment, an announcement came over the loudspeaker.

---

*He did not. Benjamin Franklin died over 150 years before we had calculators.

"All classes, please report to the all-purpose room for a surprise assembly."

"Oooooooh!"

Surprise assemblies have the perfect name, because you never know what's going to happen there. It's like opening up your birthday presents.

"Not *again*!" groaned Mr. Cooper. "Okay, pringle up, everybody!"

We lined up like Pringles and walked a million hundred miles to the all-purpose room, which we call the all-*porpoise* room even though there are no dolphins in there.*

---

*I wish there *were* dolphins in the all-purpose room. It would be like SeaWorld! But the all-purpose room is just a big room with a bunch of chairs and a stage.

We had to sit boy-girl-boy-girl to make sure that we wouldn't talk to anybody we liked. I had to sit next to Little Miss Know-It-All Andrea and her crybaby friend, Emily. Ugh, disgusting!

Everybody sat down. Mr. Cooper told us to sit up straight. So we had to sit *down* and sit *up* at the same time. That was weird.

I couldn't wait for the big surprise. We were all glued to our seats.

Well, not really. That would be weird. Why would anybody glue himself to a seat? How would you get the glue off your pants?

You'll never believe who walked out on the stage at that moment. You probably think it was our principal, Mr. Klutz. But it wasn't. So nah-nah-nah boo-boo on you. It was our science teacher, Mr. Docker!

He's weird. Mr. Docker has a car that runs on potatoes. You can read about it in a book called *Mr. Docker Is Off His Rocker!* But not now!

"Good morning, Ella Mentry students," Mr. Docker said. "Do you kids know what STEM stands for?"

"Sweet Tomato Elbow Macaroni?" some-body shouted.

"Sleeping Turtles Exit Maryland?"

"Smart Telephones Eliminate Money?"

"Stop Trying to Eat Monsters?"

"No," said Mr. Docker. "STEM stands for Science, Technology, Engineering, and Math."

"Ohhhhhh."

"I have good news and bad news for you," Mr. Docker told us. "The bad news is that our school's STEM scores are way down from last year. So I got permission from Mr. Klutz to bring in my old college roommate to help us with STEM—the world-famous scientist Dr. Melvin Snow.

Please give him a round of applause. Dr. Snow, come on out here!"

We all clapped our hands in a circle, which is what you're supposed to do any time anybody gets introduced. Nobody knows why.

Dr. Snow came out from behind the stage. He had really frizzy hair and a weird look in his eyes.

"Snowman!" said Mr. Docker as he hugged Dr. Snow. I guess that's Dr. Snow's nickname.

"That Snowman guy looks crazy," I whispered to Andrea.

"What makes you think that?" she replied.

"Look at his wild frizzy hair," I told her. "Anybody who has wild frizzy hair must be crazy."

"You shouldn't judge people by the way their hair looks, Arlo," Andrea told me. "You're just stereotyping Dr. Snow."

"How can you type on a stereo?"

"Arlo, I was beginning to think you had matured," Andrea told me. "But I guess I was wrong. When are you going to grow up?"

"In about ten years," I told her. "When are you going to grow *down*?"

Andrea rolled her eyes, so I knew I won the argument.

At that point, the weirdest thing in the history of the world happened.

The Snowman took a balloon out of his pocket and blew it up. Then he tied a knot in the end.

"Watch this," he said. "If I rub this balloon against my head, it will stick to the wall."

"Your head will stick to the wall?" I asked.

"Not my head," he replied. "I'm going to stick the *balloon* to the wall!"

Oh. That's different.

The Snowman rubbed the balloon against his frizzy hair. Then he put the balloon against the wall. And you know what? It stuck! Just like he said it would.

Everybody went "WOW," which is "MOM" upside down.

"Rubbing the balloon against my hair added electrons to the surface of the balloon," said the Snowman. "So the wall was more positively charged than the balloon. That's science!"

"Does anybody have a question for Dr. Snow?" asked Mr. Docker.

"Yeah," I said. "Why would anybody want to stick a balloon to a wall?"

"For the fun of it!" replied the Snowman. "Science is fun!"

"Any other questions?" asked Mr. Docker.

Andrea waved her hand in the air like she was washing a big window with a rag. So of *course*, she got called on.

"You said you had good news and bad news," said Andrea. "But you only told us the bad news. What's the good news?"

"Oh yes. I almost forgot," said Mr. Docker. "The good news is that Ella Mentry School is going to have a fair!"

A fair? I *love* fairs!

"Yay!" everybody shouted.

Fairs are cool. You get to play games and eat cotton candy and go on rides and win stuffed animals and—

"We're going to have a *science* fair," said the Snowman.

WHAT?!

Brainstorming

A *science* fair? I never heard of a science fair.

"Will there be cotton candy at the science fair?" asked Ryan.

"No," said the Snowman.

"Will there be rides?" asked Alexia.

"No."

"Can we win stuffed animals?" I asked.

"No."

What?! The science fair sounded like a science *unfair* to me.

"Boooooooooo!"

Everybody was booing and hooting and hollering and freaking out. Mr. Docker held up his hand and made a V with his fingers. That's the victory peace sign. It means "shut up."

"The science fair is going to be *fun*!" the Snowman told us. "Each of you can do an experiment, just like a real scientist."

"Kids can't be scientists," somebody yelled.

"Sure they can!" replied the Snowman. "You can conduct experiments in chemistry, physics, biology, and engineering using everyday objects you have around your house. Each of you will do a project."

Wait. I think he just said the *P* word.

"Project" is a horrible word because it means work. It means cutting and pasting and drawing and gluing and folding and stapling stuff. I'd rather fall into quicksand than do a project. I'd rather get attacked by a porcupine than do a project. I'd rather go to school on the *weekend* than do a project.

"Will there be prizes for the best project?" asked Andrea, who will do *anything* as long as she might win a prize so she can show that she's better than everybody else.

"Yes!" said the Snowman. "The student with the best science project will win a year's pass to the city science museum, and they will also receive a year's supply of Porky's Pork Sausages."

"Yay!" everybody started cheering.

I don't like museums very much, but Porky's Pork Sausages are the *best* pork sausages.

"Oooh, I hope I win!" said Little Miss Perfect as we filed out of the all-porpoise room.

"Me too!" said Emily, who always agrees with everything Andrea says.

When we got back to class, Mr. Cooper passed out.

I mean, he passed out paper and pencils. He told us to start taking notes and brainstorming about science fair ideas. Brainstorming is when you have a storm in your brain, so it has the perfect name.

"I need to use the restroom," he said.

"I'll be back in a few minutes to see how you're making out."

"Ugh, gross!" we all shouted.

As soon as Mr. Cooper left, Ryan, Michael, Neil, and I snapped into action. We got up on our chairs and shook our butts at the class.

"Boys!" Andrea said, rolling her eyes. "While you waste your time acting like dumbheads, I'm going to get to work so I can win the science fair contest."

I really didn't care about winning the science fair contest. I just wanted to make sure that *Andrea* didn't win. So I sat back down and tried to think of a cool science fair project.

"We should blow something up," I suggested. "Scientists are always blowing stuff up."

"Blowing things up is not science," said Little Miss Party Pooper. "Science is all about inventing new, useful things and building things that make life easier for people."

Hmmm. Inventing things. That got all of us thinking.

"I'm going to invent a solar-powered skateboard," said Alexia. "The top will be covered with solar panels."

"That's a cool idea," I said.*

---

*Using nuclear power would be even cooler, but it's hard to fit a nuclear reactor on a skateboard.

"I'm going to invent an electric chicken chucker," said Ryan.

"What does a chicken chucker do?" asked Neil.

"It chucks chickens," Ryan replied.

I don't know why chucking chickens would make anybody's life easier. It sure wouldn't make a chicken's easier. But in my head, I imagined a machine chucking chickens, and it *did* seem cool.

"I'm going to invent a time machine," said Neil. "That way, I can go back to the year before Twinkies were invented."

"Why would you want to do that?" asked Emily.

"So I could invent Twinkies!" Neil

replied. "I'll be rich, rich, rich!"

That's when I got the greatest idea in the history of the world.

"I'm going to invent an air conditioner that you wear on your feet," I said.

"Why would you want to put air conditioners on your feet?" asked Neil.

"Sometimes my feet get hot," I explained.

"I'm going to invent antigravity underwear," said Michael.

"Why?" Neil asked.

"So I can fly, of course!" said Michael.

We were all coming up with really good ideas for the science fair. I drew a picture of myself walking around with two little air conditioners on my feet.

"What are you going to do for *your* science project, Andrea?" asked Emily.

"Oh, my project is a *secret*," Andrea replied.

I tried to peek at Andrea's paper, but she was hanging all over it so I couldn't see.

"I *still* say we should blow something

up," I announced. "Maybe we can invent a robot that will make people's lives easier, and then we'll have to blow it up when the robot turns evil. I saw that in a movie once."

At that moment, the weirdest thing in the history of the world happened. I glanced toward the doorway and saw the Snowman's frizzy psycho hair in the corner. He was rubbing his hands together and listening to our conversation.

I don't care what anybody says. The Snowman is definitely crazy, and he probably wants to take over the world.

There are only two reasons why anybody ever rubs their hands together.

Either they want to take over the world, or they're cold.

And the Snowman wasn't cold.

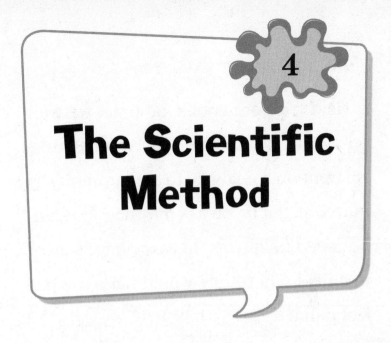

The Scientific Method

For first period the next day, we had science. When we got to the science room, the Snowman wasn't there. But Mr. Docker was.

"Follow me," he told us.

"Where are we going?" asked Emily.

"We're going on a field trip," replied Mr. Docker.

"Yay!"

Field trips are cool. One time, we went on a field trip to the zoo. Another time, we went on a field trip to a natural history museum. But if you ask me, they shouldn't be called field trips unless you take a trip to a field. Then they would have the perfect name.

Mr. Docker led us to a secret stairway near the science room. We started climbing the steps. And climbing. And *climbing*! Climbing steps is *tiring*.

"Where are we going?" asked Michael.

"You'll find out," said Mr. Docker.

I thought I was gonna die from climbing all those steps. I was huffing and

puffing and sweating and panting.*

Finally, Mr. Docker opened a door at the top of the stairs. And you'll never believe in a million hundred years what was up there.

We were on the roof of the school!

---

*That means I was wearing pants. It would be weird to climb the steps at school with no pants on.

Did you ever go out on the roof of your school? It's cool up there. It's like being on the top of the Empire State Building. You can see forever from the roof. Or at least the next block. And you'll never believe who was up there.

I'm not going to tell you.

Okay, okay, I'll tell you. It was Dr. Snow, the Snowman!

He had a rope tied to a bucket, and he was swinging the bucket around his head like a lasso.

That was weird. People who swing buckets around their heads are definitely crazy.

"Hi everybody!" said the Snowman.

"Why are you swinging a bucket around your head, Dr. Snow?" asked Ryan.

"I bet it's part of a science experiment," said Andrea.

"Right you are!" said the Snowman.

Andrea smiled the smile she smiles to let everybody know that she knows something nobody else knows. The Snowman stopped swinging the bucket around and put it on the floor.

"Now I'm going to fill this bucket up with maple syrup," he said as he took a big jug of maple syrup and poured it into the bucket.

"Why are you doing that?" I asked. "Are we having pancakes?"

"No," said the Snowman. "Now I'm

going to swing the bucket around my head again, with syrup inside it."

"Won't the syrup fly all over the place?" asked Emily. "It will be a sticky mess."

"There's only one way to find out," said the Snowman. "That's why scientists do experiments."

The Snowman picked up the bucket with the rope and started swinging it around slowly. Emily looked scared.

"I'm scared," said Emily.

"Okay, now I'm going to swing it a little faster," said the Snowman. "Stand back!"

"Watch out!" shouted Emily, covering her eyes.

"Run for your lives!" shouted Neil.

The Snowman started swinging the

bucket around faster. And faster. The bucket was flying around him sideways. The Snowman looked like one of those cowboys at a rodeo who was about to rope a steer.

And then the most amazing thing in the history of the world happened.

Nothing! The maple syrup didn't fly out of the bucket like I thought it would. It just stayed in there even though the bucket was sideways.

"WOW," we all said, which is "MOM" upside down.

"It's like magic!" I hollered.

"No, this is a demonstration of *centripetal force*," said the Snowman. "When an object is moving in a circular path, centripetal force keeps it fixed on that path."

"Cool!" we all said.

"Isn't science interesting?" asked Mr. Docker.

"When I grow up," Andrea said, "I'm going to be a scientist."

"Me too," said Emily, who always does everything Andrea does.

The Snowman kept swinging the bucket around and around. That's when the weirdest thing in the history of the world happened. I guess the rope that was attached to the bucket came loose, because the next thing anybody knew, the bucket of maple syrup went flying off the roof!

"*Ahhhhhhhhhh!*" shouted the Snowman as he fell down. He still had the rope in his hand, but the bucket was gone.

We all ran to the edge of the roof to look below. The bucket was on the grass in front of the school, and the sidewalk was covered with maple syrup.

"And *that* was a demonstration of *centrifugal* force," said the Snowman. "No worries. I'll clean that mess up later."

"I'm glad nobody was walking around down there," said Mr. Docker. "Somebody could have gotten hurt."

That was weird. But if you think *that* was weird, you'll never believe the weird thing that happened next.

I'm not going to tell you.

Okay, okay, I'll tell you. But you have to read the next chapter. So nah-nah-nah boo-boo on you.

The Great Egg Drop Challenge

There was a table on the other side of the roof with a bunch of junk on it: pieces of cloth, bubble wrap, feathers, string, straws, tape, cotton balls, rubber bands, toilet paper tubes, plastic bags, Popsicle sticks, cardboard boxes, some Styrofoam, and a big box of Honey Sugar Bongos.

Oh, and there were also two cartons of eggs. That was weird.

"Why is all this stuff up here?" asked Ryan.

"We're going to do a science project," said the Snowman. "I call it The Great Egg Drop Challenge."

"We're going to eat egg drop soup?" Ryan asked. "Yum!"

"No," said the Snowman. "We're going to drop eggs off the roof!"

He was rubbing his hands together again, a sure sign that he's crazy.

"Why is dropping eggs off the roof a science project?" asked Andrea.

"Well," said the Snowman, "if you drop

an egg off the roof onto the sidewalk below, what do you think will happen?"

"The egg will break," we all replied. Duh!

"Right!" said the Snowman. "The sidewalk is much harder than the egg's shell. So we need to think of a way to prevent the egg from breaking at the end of its fall."

"How can we do that?" asked Alexia.

"There are lots of ways," said the Snowman. "Each of you is going to design a package using the things on this table to protect your egg from a fall. We'll record the results. Then we'll discuss which packages worked, which ones didn't, and

why. That way you'll learn about gravity, velocity, inertia, and acceleration."

I didn't know what any of that stuff meant. But it didn't matter, because throwing *anything* off a roof is cool. We all got to work figuring out ways to protect our eggs.

Emily wrapped a bunch of rubber bands

around her egg. "When my egg hits the sidewalk, it will bounce," she said, "but it won't break."

Ryan put his egg in a little cardboard box and filled the box with feathers. "The feathers will cushion my egg," he said, "so it won't break when it hits the sidewalk."

Michael put his egg inside a plastic bag and surrounded the egg with foam peanuts. "My egg will move inside the bag when it hits the sidewalk," he said, "but not enough to hit the hard surface and break."

Andrea made a little parachute out of some cloth and string. Then she put her egg in a basket that hung below the parachute. "If I can make my egg fall more slowly," she said, "it won't crack when it hits the ground."

Neil wrapped his egg in bubble wrap and cotton balls. Alexia put her egg inside a piece of Styrofoam and taped it shut. I put my egg inside the box of Honey Sugar Bongos. That's my favorite cereal. The cereal has so much sugar on it, you might as well pour sugar right from a sugar bowl into your mouth.

"You all have such good ideas!" said the Snowman. "I can see how some of you could become great scientists someday."

"Is there a prize for the student whose

egg doesn't break?" asked Little Miss
I-Always-Want-to-Win-Something.

"Yes," said the Snowman. "You get to
bring your egg home with you."

"What if *all* the eggs break?" asked
Emily.

"Then lunch will be scrambled eggs

today," said the Snowman. "Are you ready?"

"Ready!" we all shouted.

"Ten . . . nine . . . eight . . ." The Snowman started counting down. "You're going to learn about Newton's First and Second Laws. . . ."

"HUH?" we all said, which is also "HUH" backward.

"Seven . . . six . . . five . . . ," the Snowman continued. "An object at rest will remain at rest unless acted on by an unbalanced force."

What?!

"Four . . . three . . . two . . . ," said the Snowman. "An object in motion continues in motion with the same speed and in the same direction unless acted upon by an unbalanced force."

I had no idea what he was talking about.

"One . . . zero . . . okay, let 'em fly!"

"Bombs away!" I shouted as I threw the box of Honey Sugar Bongos off the roof.

That's when the weirdest thing in the history of the world happened.

There was a thud down below, and then a scream.

"Eeeeeeeeeek!"

We all rushed over to the edge of the roof. And you'll never believe what we saw down on the sidewalk in front of the school.

It was Mrs. Ella Mentry, the old lady who our school was named after! She was flat on her back.

"Help!" she shouted. "I'm under attack!"

"Uh-oh," said the Snowman.

Dr. Snow and Mr. Docker went running down the stairs as fast as they could go. We all followed them. I was huffing and puffing and sweating and panting when we got down to the first floor. Then we ran out the front door of the school.

Mrs. Mentry was still lying on the ground. Her eyes were closed, and she had pieces of egg all over her.

"Oh no," shouted Alexia. "Ella Mentry is dead!"

"We killed her!" shouted Neil.

Everybody was yelling and screaming and freaking out.*

But Mrs. Mentry wasn't dead, and we didn't kill her. I know that for sure, because after a few seconds her eyes opened.

"Are you okay, Mrs. Mentry?" asked Mr. Docker.

"No, I'm *not* okay!" shouted Mrs. Mentry angrily. "What idiot spread maple syrup all over the sidewalk? I think my leg may be broken!"

"I was trying to teach the students about centripetal force," explained the Snowman.

---

*My mom told me that too many eggs are bad for your health. Now I see she was right.

"By putting maple syrup on the side-walk!?" shouted Mrs. Mentry.

"B-b-but . . . ," said the Snowman and Mr. Docker.

I started giggling because they both said "but," which sounds just like "butt" even though it only has one *t.*

"And what did you teach the students by throwing eggs off the roof?" shouted Mrs. Mentry as she removed a piece of eggshell from her face.

"Uh . . . gravity, velocity, acceleration—"

"Isn't there some *other* way to teach those things?" shouted Mrs. Mentry. "I got hit on the head with a box of Honey Sugar Bongos!"

Everybody looked at me because they knew I threw the box of Honey Sugar Bongos off the roof.

I was wondering what happened to my egg. If Ella Mentry's head was softer than the sidewalk, maybe my egg didn't crack when the box of Honey Sugar Bongos landed on her. But this didn't seem like the right time to open the box and find out.

"Why is it that every time I come to this school I get attacked by flying food?" shouted Ella Mentry.

"B-b-but . . . ," said the Snowman and Mr. Docker.

"That's it!" said Mrs. Mentry. "Get me

out of here! I need to call my lawyer! This is the last straw!"

Huh? I didn't know we ran out of straws. What did straws have to do with anything anyway?

"B-b-but . . ."

"I didn't donate a million dollars to this school so the students could throw food at me every time I visit!" Mrs. Mentry shouted. "I want my money back!"

"B-b-but . . ."

They sure say "but" a lot.

Getting Dirt on Dr. Snow

Mrs. Mentry was *really* mad when all those eggs landed on her. We tried to pick the shells out of her clothes, but she was a gooey mess. I guess the yolk was on her!

It looked like she was going to totally freak out, but you'll never believe who came running out of the school at that moment.

It was Mr. Klutz, our principal! He has no hair at all. I mean *none*. If they gave out prizes to people who have the least amount of hair, Mr. Klutz would win.

"I am *soooooo* sorry!" Mr. Klutz said to Ella Mentry.

"I want my money back," she barked as she brushed more eggshells off her dress. "I slipped on maple syrup and was attacked by flying eggs! Take my name off the front of the building! You owe me a million dollars! You're lucky I don't sue!"

"Now, now, Mrs. Mentry," said Mr. Klutz. "There, there."

Grown-ups always say "now now" and "there there" when they want to calm down an angry person. Nobody knows why.

But I guess it must have worked, because Mrs. Mentry calmed down. An ambulance came to take her to the hospital. Before it drove away, Mr. Klutz promised her that she would *never* get attacked by flying food again. He also invited her to be his special guest at the science fair.

"*Please* don't make us give back the million dollars," begged Mr. Klutz. "We need that money. It's for . . . the *children*."

He was making a sad puppy dog face, so we knew he was really desperate.*

---

*If you're ever really desperate, just make a sad puppy dog face. Even grown-ups do it. It works every time.

"I'll think about it," Mrs. Mentry said. She was still mad.

After that, we went inside for lunch. Everybody felt bad about what happened to Mrs.

Mentry. I felt worse than anyone because I'm the one who hit her in the head with a box of Honey Sugar Bongos. I wanted to go to Antarctica and live with the penguins.

Nobody was talking much while we ate our peanut butter and jelly sandwiches. It was quiet in the vomitorium. After lunch, we went out for recess, but nobody was in the mood to play.

"What do you want to do?" Ryan asked.

"I don't know," said Michael. "What do *you* want to do?"

"Let's play Talk Like a Grown-up," I suggested.

Talk Like a Grown-up is one of my favorite games. All you have to do is talk like a grown-up, so it has the perfect name.

"You start, A.J.," said Alexia.

"Nice weather we're having," I said.

"It's lovely," said Alexia. "They say it may rain on Friday."

"How is your lawn?" asked Neil. "Mine needs watering."

"I want more money," I said.

"You're fired!" said Alexia.

"I need to lose ten pounds," said Ryan, "and my hair is falling out."

"If I don't get coffee, I'll die," said Michael.

"Do you want to play golf?" asked Alexia.

"Not now," I said. "I have to read the newspaper."

"My back hurts," said Neil.

"My feet hurt," said Michael.

"*Everything* hurts," said Alexia.

"I need to trim my nose hair," I said.

Man, talking like a grown-up is boring. I hope I never grow up to be a grown-up.

Little Miss Perfect and her crybaby friend, Emily, must have been listening, because they came over to annoy us, as usual.

"It's not nice to make fun of grown-ups," said Andrea. "*You'll* be a grown-up some-day, Arlo."

"No way!" I insisted.

"Grown-ups are weird," said Ryan.

"Speaking of weird grown-ups," said Alexia, "what's the deal with Dr. Snow?"

"I don't trust that guy," I said. "I still say he's crazy, with that frizzy psycho hair and those crazy eyes. I think he wants to take over the world."

"That's ridiculous, Arlo," said Andrea. "Stop trying to scare Emily."

"I'm scared," said Emily.

"Maybe he had us attack Mrs. Mentry with eggs on *purpose*," Alexia suggested.

"Did you ever think of that? Maybe it wasn't a science project at all."

"Yeah," I told the group. "That was just the *beginning* of his secret plan for world-wide domination."

"We've got to *do* something!" shouted Emily, and then she ran away.

"Dr. Snow has got to go," I said.

Then I got up and started chanting "DR. SNOW HAS GOT TO GO! DR. SNOW HAS GOT TO GO!"

I thought everybody was going to get up and start chanting with me. But nobody got up. Nobody started chanting. I hate when that happens.

"A.J., if what you say is true," said Alexia, "there's only one thing we can do."

"What's that?"

"We've got to get some dirt on Dr. Snow," Alexia told me.

"Why would we want to get dirt on him?" I asked. "Then he'd just be covered with dirt."

Andrea rolled her eyes. "Alexia means we should find out some bad things that Dr. Snow did," said Andrea. "Then we can blackmail him."

"What's blackmail?" asked Michael.

"That's what grown-ups do to people when they find out bad things about them," said Andrea.

"We should sneak around and stalk the Snowman," said Neil. "Maybe we can catch him red-handed doing bad things."

Neil should get the Nobel Prize. That's a prize they give out to people who don't have bells.

Sneaking around is cool. We snuck around the playground fence until we reached the back door of the school. Then we snuck inside like we were secret agents, hugging the walls and looking in both directions to make sure nobody was following us.

"We should be wearing night vision goggles," I whispered.

"Why?" asked Neil. "It's daytime."

"Who cares?" I replied. "Night vision goggles are cool."

We snuck up and down the hallways

looking for the Snowman, but we couldn't find him.

"He's probably hiding in a secret lab where he does his evil experiments," I whispered.

We passed by the teachers' lounge. That's a room where no kids are allowed, but the teachers can get pedicures and play Ping-Pong all day. I peeked through the little window in the door.

That's when I saw him. The Snowman! He was sitting all by himself.

"*Pssssst*! He's in *here*!" I whispered.

"Okay, what's the plan?" whispered Alexia.

"*This* is the plan," I said. Then I yanked

open the door and burst into the teachers' lounge.

"Freeze, dirtbag!" I shouted.

That's what policemen always shout on TV when they sneak up on bad guys. Nobody knows why.

The Snowman was completely surprised. He dropped his sandwich onto the floor.

"Aha!" I shouted. "We caught you red-handed, Snowman!"

"I beg your pardon?" the Snowman asked.

"I have one question for you," I told him. "Do you have any bells?"

"Uh, I have a doorbell at my house," said

the Snowman. "Why do you ask?"

"Just as I suspected!" I said. "You *can't* be a real scientist. They give the Nobel Prize to scientists who don't have bells.

But you have a bell, so that proves that you're not a real scientist. You're a fake. A phony!"

"Are you kids allowed to be in the teachers' lounge?" asked Dr. Snow. "Shouldn't you be at recess?"

"Stop trying to change the subject, Snowman!" I barked. "What are *you* doing in here?"

"I was *trying* to eat my lunch," he replied, picking his sandwich up off the floor.

"Yeah, *sure*," I told him. "That's what they *all* say. We know what you're up to, Snowman. You planned that attack on Mrs. Mentry so you could shut down the school. It's all part of your evil plot to take over the world!"

"What?!" he said. "B-b-but . . ."

We all started giggling because he said "butt" with one *t*.

"Dr. Snow was just eating his lunch, Arlo," said Andrea. "Now you're being ridiculous."

Maybe so, but I still didn't trust him. Neither did Alexia.

"I've got my eye on you, Snowman!" she said.

That was weird. Why would you want to put your eye on somebody? That's kind of gross.

Galileo in the Library

So we still had to get some dirt on the Snowman. But how?

"We need to play it cool," Alexia said. "Let's just pretend everything is normal. The Snowman will show his true colors. Then we can nail him."

Huh? What do colors have to do with anything? People talk funny.

That afternoon, we had library class with Mrs. Roopy. We walked a million hundred miles to the media center, which used to be called the library before they changed the name. Nobody knows why.

When we got to the media center, Mrs. Roopy wasn't there. Instead, there was some guy who looked a lot like Mrs. Roopy with a beard. She's always pretending to be somebody else. One time, she dressed up like Neil Armstrong. Mrs. Roopy is loopy.

"Why do you have a beard today, Mrs. Roopy?" Ryan asked.

"Who's Mrs. Roopy?" said Mrs. Roopy. "I'm Galileo, the famous sixteenth-century scientist."

"Wait," I said. "You only have one name?"

"No," said Galileo. "Galileo is just my first name."

"So what's your last name?" asked Andrea.

"Galilei," said Galileo.

"Your first name is Galileo and your last name is Galilei?" asked Michael.

"That's right," said Galileo Galilei. "It sounded so nice, my parents made it my name twice. I'm surprised you never heard of me. I discovered the moons of Jupiter and the rings of Saturn with my early telescope. I was the first person to see craters on the moon. I'm from Italy."

"I like pizza," said Ryan.

"*Everybody* likes pizza," said Galileo. "Hey, I hear you're going to have a science fair next week."

"Yes," said Andrea. "Each of us has to make a science project."

"Well, you came to the right place," said Galileo. "There are lots of books in the media center filled with fun science projects for kids."

Galileo passed out a bunch of books for us to look over.

"Oh, cool!" said Neil. "It says here that you can build a catapult with just a plastic spoon, some rubber bands, and Popsicle sticks. It shoots marshmallows!"

"That would make a great project for the science fair," said Galileo. "You know, science is all about asking 'why' questions. Why is the sky blue? Why do fish swim and birds fly? Can any of you think of a why question?"

"Yeah," I said, "why do we have to do a science project?"

Galileo passed out.

I mean, he passed out pencils and papers so we could take notes and draw pictures for our science projects.

"I'm going to build a pasta rocket," said Ryan. "It uses uncooked pasta, mouthwash, and yeast for fuel."

"I'm going to build a fizz inflator," said Michael. "I just need to put baking soda and vinegar in a soda bottle and attach a balloon to the end to inflate it. The reaction makes carbon dioxide to inflate the balloon."

"I'm going to build an exploding lunch bag," said Alexia. "You just take a Ziploc freezer bag and fill it with warm water, baking soda, and vinegar."

"I'm going to build a flying drone," I said.

Drones are cool. I always wanted to have my own drone.

I was drawing a picture of my drone when I got another great idea. I could attach some Porky's Pork Sausages to the bottom of my drone so it could deliver sausages by air. Then you wouldn't have to go to the supermarket when you're in the mood for a pork sausage. It was genius!*

---

*Maybe doing a project with Porky's Pork Sausages would help me win the grand prize and make Andrea lose.

"What are you going to make for *your* science project, Andrea?" asked Emily.

Andrea was covering her worksheet with her hands so nobody could see it.

"I'm working on a *secret* science project," she said mysteriously.

"Oooh, what is it?" Emily asked.

"If I told you, it wouldn't be a secret," Andrea replied.

Andrea will do *anything* to win the grand prize at the science fair. She's afraid that one of us is going to try and steal her idea. What is her problem?

We were all drawing pictures and making lists of materials we were going to need for our science projects. And you'll never believe who walked through the door at that moment.

Nobody! You can't walk through a door. Doors are made of wood. But you'll never believe who walked through the door*way*.

It was the Snowman! He was holding a machine that looked like a leaf blower.

"Dr. Snow!" said Galileo. "To what do we owe the pleasure of your company?"

That's grown-up talk for "What are *you* doing here?"

"I wanted to see what projects the students were planning for the science fair," the Snowman replied. "But first, take a look at my new invention."

He pulled a rope, and the engine on the leaf blower roared to life. It was loud! A blast of air shot out the end.

"WOW," we all said, which is "MOM" upside down.

"That's a cool leaf blower, Dr. Snow," said Andrea.

"Oh, it's not a leaf blower," said the Snowman. "I call it the Birthday Blower. It's a

machine for blowing out birthday candles. You know how it's hard to blow out that last candle on your birthday cake? If you have a Birthday Blower, it blows the candles out *for* you!"

"That is cool," I said, even though I didn't think it was all that cool.

The Snowman walked around the class and looked at what each of us was planning for the science fair. Neil described his rubber band–powered catapult that shoots marshmallows.

"Yes! Yes! Yes!" shouted the Snowman.

Ryan described his pasta rocket.

"Excellent!" shouted the Snowman.

Alexia described her exploding Ziploc lunch bag.

"Perfect!" shouted the Snowman.

Michael described his fizz inflator.

"Fascinating!" shouted the Snowman.

I described my remote-controlled flying sausage delivery drone.

"Genius!" shouted the Snowman.

The Snowman loved all our science fair projects. Well, except for Andrea's secret project, of course. She wouldn't let him see what she was working on.

"Yes! Yes! Yes!" shouted the Snowman, rubbing his hands together. "This is going to be the greatest science fair in the history of science fairs!"

Welcome to the Science Fair

We spent the next week making our projects. My mom and dad helped me build my remote-controlled flying sausage delivery drone. It was the coolest. It *had* to be cooler than the secret lame project Andrea was working on.

Finally, it was the day of the science fair.

When I got to school, there was electricity in the air.

Well, not really. If there was electricity in the air, we would all get electrocuted.

But all our parents and teachers were there. Galileo was there. The owner of Porky's Pork Sausages, Peter Porky, was there. And of course, Mrs. Ella Mentry was there. She was walking with crutches because she'd hurt her leg in the Great Egg Drop Challenge. The walls of the gym were covered with science posters and banners.

Before the opening ceremony, we got to walk around and look at all the science projects. One girl made a periscope out of a milk carton. Some boy made a hoverboard. Somebody else made fossils out of bread and gummy bears.

A fifth grader used a lemon to make electricity. A fourth grader made a fountain out of soda and Mentos. Somebody made a rotten egg stink bomb. It was cool.

There were solar ovens, weather stations, balloon rockets, levitating magnets, exploding toothpaste, and glow-in-the-dark slime. Kids had created projects using Jell-O, paper airplanes, Silly Putty, invisible ink, Play-Doh, lava lamps, and walkie-talkies.

"Yes! Yes! Yes!" the Snowman said as he walked around the gym. "I love it!"

Andrea's project was a big secret, but now she had to show everybody what it was. She pulled a sheet off the table, and you'll never believe in a million hundred years what she had under there.

It was a volcano!

"I made it out of papier-mâché," Andrea announced. "When it erupts, lava will shoot out of it."

Oh, *man*! Why didn't I think of that? Andrea was *sure* to win the grand prize with an erupting volcano. She always wins everything. Why can't a volcano erupt on Andrea's head?

Everybody in the gym was buzzing. Well, not really. We're not bees. Mr. Klutz

stepped up to the microphone and made the shut-up peace sign with his fingers. Everybody stopped talking.

"Welcome to the Ella Mentry School science fair," Mr. Klutz announced. "Blah blah blah blah young future scientists blah blah blah blah unlock the secrets of the universe blah blah blah blah thank Dr. Snow for organizing blah blah blah blah our special guest, Mrs. Ella Mentry, blah blah blah blah . . ."

He went on like that for a million hundred minutes. What a snoozefest. Finally, he stopped talking.

"Let the science fair begin!" announced the Snowman. "A.J., start things off!

Andrea, you can warm up your volcano now."

"Sure thing!" we said.

I flipped the switch on the remote control. The rotors on my drone started to spin. The drone rose up in the air over everyone's head.

"What a great idea!" said Peter Porky. "This could be a good way to deliver Porky's Pork Sausages."

Red-hot lava started to bubble up at the top of Andrea's volcano.

"Ooooo! Ahhhh!" everybody oooed and ahhhed.

"Neil, show us how your catapult works," said the Snowman.

Neil put a marshmallow on the spoon and pulled the spoon back. Then he let go, and the marshmallow went flying.

That's when the weirdest thing in the history of the world happened. Neil's marshmallow hit one of the rotors on my drone. The drone started spinning and flying crazily.

"Watch out!" somebody yelled.

My drone swooped down and knocked over Michael's fizz inflator!

The fizz inflator fell on top of Alexia's exploding lunch bag! It exploded!

That set off Ryan's pasta rocket, which flew up and knocked out another one of the rotors on my drone! The drone was

zooming all over the place! People were diving for cover!

"It's out of control!" shouted Andrea.

"Run for your lives!" shouted Neil.

"Call 911!" somebody shouted.

That's when something even *weirder* happened.

"I love it!" shouted the Snowman, rubbing his hands together. "It's all going according to plan! Bwahahaha! I'm going to take over the world! Bwahahaha!"*

"See, I *told* you he was crazy!" I said to Andrea.

"I *knew* he would show his true colors!" said Alexia.

---

*Any time somebody says "Bwahahaha" while they're laughing, you know they're crazy. Normal people never say "Bwahahaha." That's the first rule of being normal.

My drone was hovering right above Andrea's volcano.

"Release the sausages, A.J.!" shouted Mr. Klutz. "Your drone is too heavy! It's going to crash and hurt somebody!"

I flipped the switch that made the Porky's Pork Sausages slide off the bottom of my drone.

The sausages dropped right into the middle of Andrea's volcano!

"Oh no!" shouted Andrea. "Arlo, you ruined my science project!"

"The volcano is full of dangerous chemicals!" shouted Andrea's father.

"It's gonna blow!" somebody yelled.

The next thing we knew, six pork sausages came flying out of the volcano! One

of them hit Ella Mentry, and she fell down.

"I'm being attacked with food again!" she yelled. "Owww! My leg!"

One of the flying sausages was about to hit Mr. Klutz on the head, but he dived out of the way and crashed into our vice principal, Mrs. Jafee! The two of them fell on a table, and the table collapsed under their weight!

Everybody was yelling and screaming and hooting and hollering and freaking out!

"Yes! Yes! Yes!" shouted the Snowman. "It's all part of my master plan. I will rule the world! Bwahahaha! Nothing can stop me! Bwahahaha!"

I heard a siren outside.

"Uh-oh," said the Snowman as he

headed for the door. "I must escape to my secret lab and conduct evil experiments."

"Not so fast, buster!" shouted Mrs. Mentry.

She stuck out one of her crutches and tripped the Snowman with it. Galileo tackled him and wrestled him to the ground.

"Let me go!" shouted the Snowman. "I must take over the world!"

"Hold that man!" shouted Mrs. Mentry. "First he attacked me with eggs and now pork sausages. That's the last straw!"

Why is she always talking about straws? You'd think that the school would just buy extra straws so we wouldn't be running out of them all the time.

At that moment, the outside doors opened and four guys wearing white coats came running in.

"Who's in charge here?" one of them shouted.

Our principal and vice principal were unconscious under the table they fell on.

"I'm in charge!" said Mrs. Mentry. "My name is Ella Mentry. The school is named after me."

"We got a report that some mad scientist was trying to take over the world," the guy in the white coat said.

"Here's your man," Mrs. Mentry said, pointing at the Snowman. "Take him away, boys."

Well, that's pretty much what happened. We never did find out who won the science fair. The men in white coats carried the Snowman out to an ambulance and drove away. When it was all over, Mrs. Mentry recovered and donated a million dollars to build the Ella Mentry Hospital for Frizzy-Haired Mad Scientists Who Rub Their Hands Together and Want to Take Over the World.

Maybe next year, we'll have a plain old fair with cotton candy, rides, and stuffed animals. Maybe we'll throw eggs off the roof of the school again. Maybe a meteorite will crash through the window and knock over Mr. Cooper. Maybe we'll get some dolphins in the all-porpoise room. Maybe the Snowman will stick his head to the wall. Maybe Ella Mentry will be attacked by flying food again and demand to get her money back. Maybe grown-ups will stop saying "now now" and "there there." Maybe Michael will invent anti-gravity underwear.

But it won't be easy!